D1307669

No moa, no moa,
In old Ao-tea-roa.
Can't get 'em.
They've et 'em.
They've gone
and there ain't no moa!

- New Zealand Folk Song

THE

LANDMARK EDITIONS, INC.

P.O. Box 270169 • 1402 Kansas Avenue • Kansas City, Missouri 64127
(816) 241-4919

MOAS

WRITTEN AND ILLUSTRATED BY
KATIE BECK

Dedicated to:
My wonderful teachers, friends,
and family, both immediate and extended;
and especially to my mother, Brenda,
who always encouraged me to exercise my gifts.

COPYRIGHT © 1999 BY KATIE BECK

International Standard Book Number: 0-933849-73-7 (LIB.BDG.)

Library of Congress Cataloging-in-Publication Data
Beck, Katie, 1981-
      The moas / written and illustrated by Katie Beck
      p.   cm.
      Summary: Moki, one of the moa birds being hunted into extinction
by the Maoris on New Zealand, tries to regain their lost ability to fly so
that he can escape death. Includes facts about New Zealand, the Maoris,
and the moas.
ISBN 0-933849-73-7 (lib.bdg. : alk. paper)
[1. Moas—Fiction.   2. Extinction (Biology)—Fiction.
 3. Flight—Fiction.   4. Maori (New Zealand people)—Fiction.
 5. New Zealand—Fiction.]

I. Title.
PZ7.B3807685Mo   1999
[Fic]—dc21   99-18079
                                                        CIP

Creative Coordinator: David Melton
Editorial Coordinator: Nancy R. Thatch
Computer Graphics Coordinator: Brian Hubbard

Printed in the United States of America

Landmark Editions, Inc.
P.O. Box 270169
1402 Kansas Avenue
Kansas City, Missouri 64127
(816) 241-4919

Visit our Website — www.LandmarkEditions.com

THE MOAS

As a writer and an illustrator, I know how important it is for young authors and artists to read books of different genres and see books that are illustrated in a variety of media and styles. I am very pleased that Landmark's BOOKS FOR STUDENTS BY STUDENTS® provide such a wide range of literary examples and visual experiences for creative young people to read and see.

Landmark has published autobiographies, fiction, non-fiction, science fiction, fiction-based-on-fact, fantasy, whimsy, poetry, and so on. Our books contain illustrations rendered in a broad selection of media, including watercolors, felt tips, tempera, gouache, colored pencils, pen and ink, and photographs. Some of the approaches are realistic; some are impressionistic. Others are stylized or delineated in cartoon.

I enjoy seeing most kinds of art, but I especially enjoy looking at wonderfully composed pencil illustrations. When they are done really well, pencil illustrations dazzle me.

The first time I saw Katie Beck's beautiful book, THE MOAS, with its outstanding pencil illustrations, I was dazzled. And everyone else in our offices who saw them responded with *oohs* and *aahs*. I was not surprised when her book won The National Written and Illustrated by... Award in the 14 to 19 Age Category.

While Katie prepared the final illustrations for the publication of her book, she expanded and improved all of her drawings. The new ones became even more spectacular.

I thoroughly enjoyed working with Katie! She is a very sweet, polite, and sensitive young woman, who is eager to please. More importantly, she is willing to challenge her abilities and work hard to widen her range of skills as an artist.

Katie writes beautifully, too. With a strong sense of how pictures and words should become one, she tells her story simply, but eloquently, allowing her illustrations to interact with the narrative, as they should in a good picture-story book.

I like the story of THE MOAS very much. And as I have already told you, I am a "pencil freak." I am completely dazzled by Katie's exceptional illustrations.

I think you are sure to enjoy them, too. So as you turn the pages of this beautiful book, prepare to be dazzled.

— David Melton
Creative Coordinator
Landmark Editions, Inc.

A long, long time ago, a flock of very large birds flew across the Pacific Ocean. After traveling for hundreds of miles, they landed on the shore of a beautiful island that would later become part of New Zealand.

The moas, as they would one day be called, were magnificent birds that stood nearly twice as high as an ordinary man. Their strong, slender legs could carry them swiftly across the ground. And their huge wings could lift their slim, graceful bodies high into the air.

As the moas rested after their tiring journey, they looked around at their new surroundings. They saw plenty of tender green leaves and tasty berries to eat.

"What a wonderful place!" they said.

Better still, they saw no fierce predators that would hunt them and try to kill them.

"At last we have come to a land where we have nothing to fear!" they said joyfully.

The moas happily preened their beautiful feathers. Then they folded their enormous wings and made themselves at home in the lush paradise they had found.

New Zealand — a country made up of two large islands and several smaller ones, which lie in the Southwest Pacific Ocean. New Zealand is located about 1,200 miles southeast of Australia.

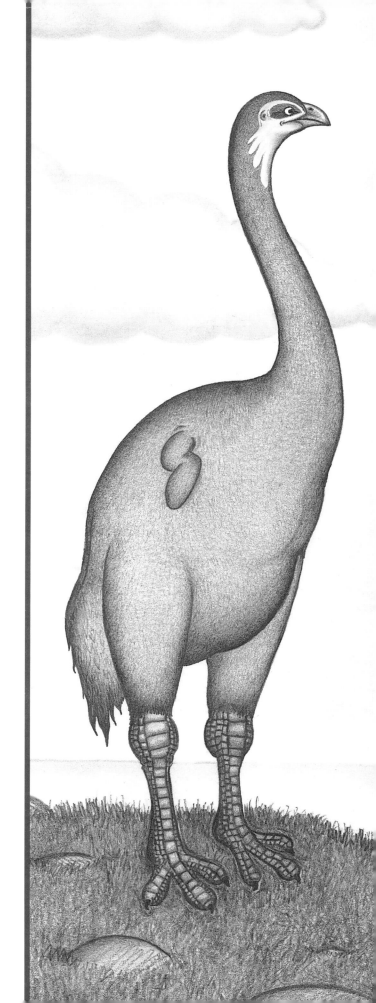

For many, many years, the moas lived peacefully on the island. Every day they feasted on delicious plants. They drank clear, fresh water from the streams. And they relaxed in the warmth of the bright sunlight.

In fact, the moas allowed themselves to relax too much. Over the years, their once graceful bodies became fat, and their strong, swift legs became flabby and slow. With no predators to threaten them, the moas grew lazy, too. They felt no need to exercise their great feathered wings, and eventually, they even forgot how to fly.

As time passed, their unused wings became smaller and smaller. Finally, they had nothing left but a pair of tiny stubs where their once powerful wings had been.

But the moas didn't care. They believed they were safe from danger. They thought they would never need their wings again.

Moa — a large, awkward bird that could not fly, either because it had no wings or very small ones. An adult moa stood ten to twelve feet in height. The moas were vegetarians. They built their nests on the ground out of grass, dirt, and leaves.

Then, one day as the moas were walking about, they looked out at the ocean. They saw some strange-looking creatures were moving across the water.

"What animals are those?" one moa asked.

"I don't know," replied another, "but they can swim very fast."

The birds watched in amazement as the mysterious strangers came closer and closer, and finally came ashore.

The strangers were, in fact, human beings, who were known as the Maoris. They had sailed from a distant island in Polynesia and were the first of their tribe to set foot on the coastline of New Zealand.

The curious moas had never seen human beings, so they were not in the least afraid of the Maoris. But that changed quickly when the fierce Maoris came running up from the beach, shouting wildly and waving clubs and sharp spears.

The moas were terrified! They screeched and tried to run away and hide. But they were so fat and clumsy, they couldn't move fast enough. They couldn't fly away either because their wings were too small. So the Maoris soon overtook the slowest birds and struck them down with their weapons.

Maoris — a Polynesian people who are related to Hawaiians and other South Pacific islanders. The Maoris arrived in New Zealand by canoe in the 1300s. They were known to be the fiercest natives in the South Pacific and waged war with other tribes. Today, the descendants of the Maoris speak fluent English and live peacefully among the other people of New Zealand. But they still have great pride in their cultural heritage. At ceremonial gatherings, they speak the Maori language and wear traditional Maori clothing.

The Maoris were pleased. They thought this had been the most successful hunt they had ever had. That night the tribe assembled for a great celebration.

They decorated their hair and clothing with beautiful feathers they had plucked from the moas. They ate roasted moa meat and eggs the size of watermelons, fresh from the moa nests that the birds had built on the ground. As they feasted, their tattooed faces glistened in the light of the bonfires.

When the Maoris had eaten their fill, they talked about the wonderful place they had found and how good the meat of the moas tasted. And since there were so many of the giant birds on the island, the Maoris decided to stay there.

Tattoo — a mark or design made by punching holes in the skin and inserting permanent color into them. The Maoris tattooed their faces with elaborate designs by rubbing blue coloring into grooves they had carved into their skin with knives. Their tattoos were called *mokos*. Some people thought these tattoos made them look beautiful. Others thought the designs made them look frightening.

The Maoris lived on the island for many years. They ate the fruits and vegetables that grew in abundance. Whenever they needed a fresh supply of meat, they hunted the moas. And if they wanted more large eggs, they took them from the moa nests.

The moas were always in danger. They tried to hide among the dense trees and bushes. But the Maoris were skillful hunters who knew how to track the moas and where to find their eggs.

The hunting and killing of the moas went on for many years. One by one, the number of moas dwindled until only a small flock of the birds was left on the island.

Maori Life — The Maoris were great sailors, hunters, and fishermen. Many of them were farmers as well. They also were very skilled woodcarvers who decorated their homes, war canoes, and weapons with intricately carved designs.

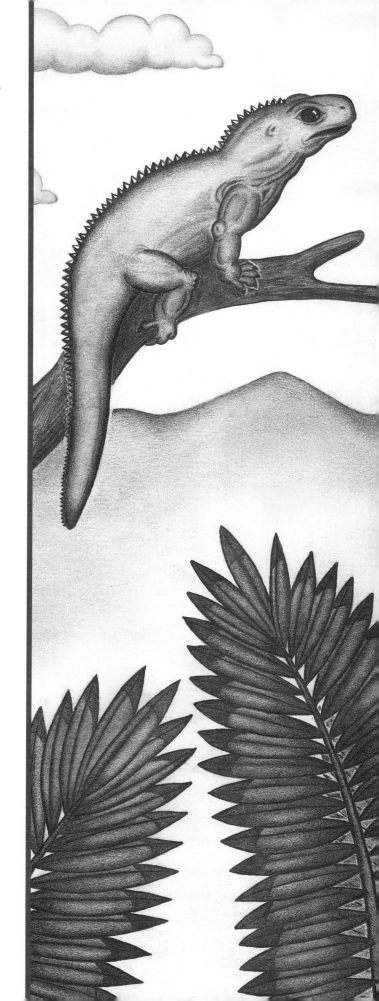

One of the moas, whose name was Moki, wanted to find a way to escape from the Maoris. One day he went deep into the forest to seek the advice of the tuatara, an ancient reptile whose wisdom was well known throughout the island.

When the tuatara saw Moki, the reptile gazed at him through a pair of intelligent black eyes that sparkled like dewdrops.

"What do you want?" asked the tuatara.

"Please, sir, could you tell me why I can't escape from the human beings?" Moki asked.

"Well," replied the tuatara in an all-knowing voice, "in the beginning, when the world was young, every kind of animal was given a special gift. We tuataras were given sharp teeth and claws to defend ourselves from predators. Through the years, we were careful to keep our teeth and claws sharp at all times.

"You moas had a special gift, too," he said. "You were given large wings that could lift you high into the air where your enemies could not reach you. But you became lazy and did not use your special gift, so your wings became very small. Now that you need them, your wings are not large enough to carry you away to safety."

"But, what can I do now?" asked Moki.

The tuatara did not answer. Instead, the old reptile closed his scaly eyelids, and he went to sleep.

Tuatara — a prehistoric reptile whose descendants still live in New Zealand. This lizardlike creature is the only living member of a group of reptiles that appeared on Earth more than 200 million years ago. It hunts insects, amphibians, snails, birds, and small lizards.

16

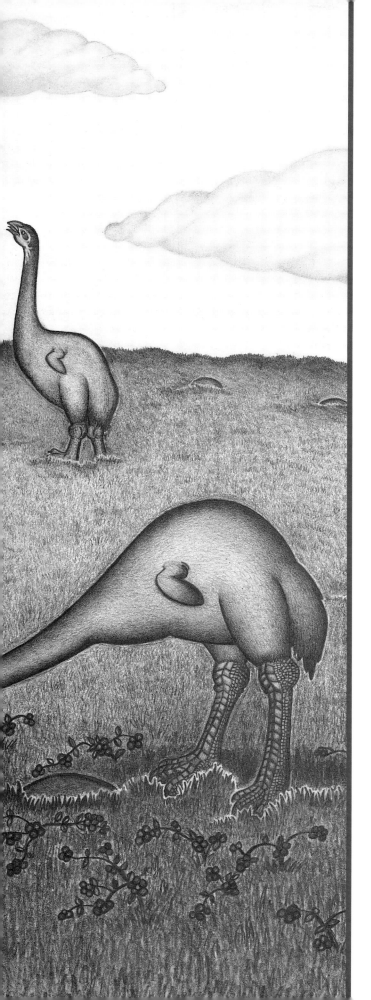

For several days, Moki thought about what the tuatara had told him. Finally, he decided what he must do.

With great determination, Moki climbed onto a big rock that stood at the top of the highest hill. Then, taking a deep breath, he began to move his little stubs up and down.

Before long some of the other moas saw Moki on the rock, and they started to gather around him.

"What are you doing?" they asked.

"I'm exercising," he replied, "so I can fly away and escape from the humans."

When the moas heard what Moki said, they laughed and laughed.

"You silly bird!" they scolded. "Don't you know that moas can't fly? Stop that useless exercising! Get something to eat before the humans come hunting for us again."

But Moki would not listen to them.

After a while, the birds grew tired of trying to get Moki to take their advice. They began stuffing themselves with fresh berries and giggling foolishly as they waddled around.

Moki continued to exercise every day. As the days passed, his body became slimmer, his legs grew stronger, and his tiny stubs moved with greater ease.

After many months had gone by, Moki's tiny stubs began to develop into wings — not big wings, but wings nevertheless. And his wings kept growing larger and stronger.

Then, one day as Moki was exercising, he felt his body slowly rise a few inches above the rock. His heart pounded with joy! Each time he flapped his wings, he was able to rise a little higher into the air.

The other moas couldn't help but notice that Moki now had wings.

"Look at Moki's funny little wings!" said one of the moas. "He's actually trying to fly with them!"

"He may have wings," said another moa, "but they will *never* be large enough to carry him away."

"Never!" chorused the other birds, and they laughed again.

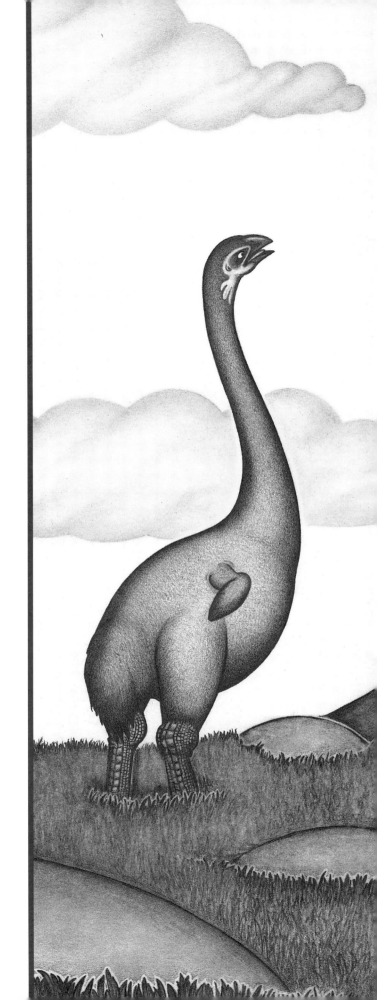

In the following weeks, Moki exercised even more. Then, one day to his delight, his wings finally were large enough to lift him into the air!

Moki let out a great cry of joy as he stretched out his beautiful new wings! Then, giving himself a mighty push with his strong legs, he lifted off and floated high above the rock. He felt the warmth of the sun on his new flight features as he rose higher and higher. He was airborne!

When the other moas looked up, they were surprised to see that Moki was soaring above their heads.

"Look at that!" one of them squawked. "Moki is *really* flying!"

"And he's leaving the island!" another exclaimed. "He's flying away to where the humans can't find him!"

"Maybe we should exercise our stubs, too," one young moa said thoughtfully.

"Nonsense!" sneered an older bird. "That would be far too much work. Besides, the humans will never find all of us."

"That's right," they all agreed smugly.

The Maori hunters did not kill all of the moas at once. But day after day, and month after month, and year after year, they kept on hunting the birds. After each hunt, they celebrated by roasting the meat of another moa and eating more of the moa eggs.

From time to time, the Maoris did notice that there were fewer and fewer moas on the island. But that did not worry them.

"There will always be enough of the birds for us to eat," they kept telling themselves.

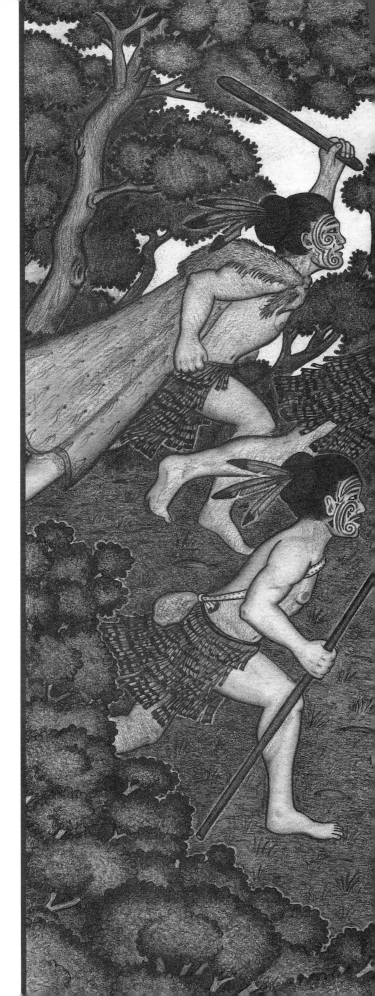

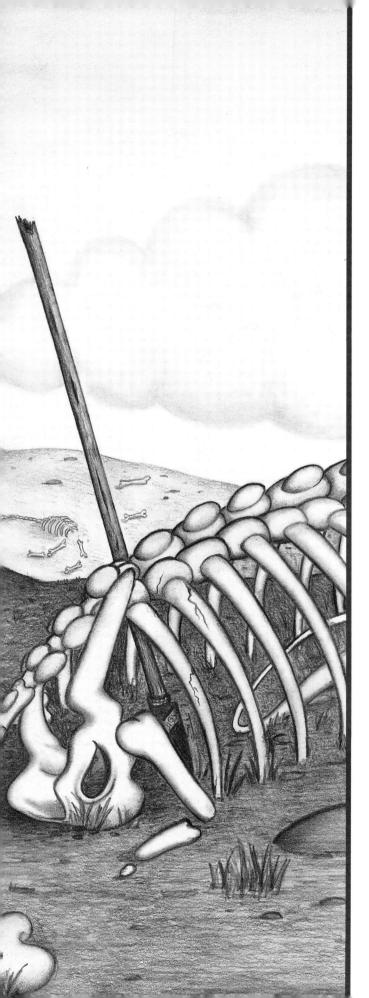

Time would prove the Maoris wrong. There finally came the day when they hunted and killed the last moa. The magnificent birds were extinct — they were gone forever.

Nothing was left of the moas except for their large bones, their crumpled feathers, and some of their broken eggshells — sorrowful reminders of an extraordinary species of bird that once had thrived on an island in New Zealand.

It was difficult for the Maoris to adjust to life without the moas, but they managed to survive on other foods. Many of them even became farmers.

But the Maoris never forgot the great birds. In times of famine or hardship, the Maoris would say:

"Ka ngaro I re ngaro a te moa."

In the Maori language it means:

"We are lost as the moa is lost."

When European settlers arrived in New Zealand, the Maoris told them the long and sad story of why so many large bones were scattered about the island.

Scientists were fascinated with the bones of the large birds. They wanted to study all the bones they could find. They kept telling the Maoris to bring them **_more_**. The Maoris, who could not speak English very well, thought the scientists were saying, **_moa_**.

So the Maoris began calling this extinct bird **_moa_**. And that is what these birds have been called ever since.

The Extinct Moas — By the 1600s the Maoris had killed all of the moas. Today, the remains of the moas can still be found, usually in swampy areas or at old Maori cooking sites.

And what became of Moki — the one moa that had flown away?

No one knows for sure. But there is a legend that says this very brave and determined bird followed the sun westward, until he came to the great land of Australia.

It has been rumored that Moki is living somewhere in the Australian Outback, where he is teaching a flock of emus how to fly.

Australia — is the smallest continent in the world, and it is the only continent that is also a country. It is located just south of the Equator and lies between the Indian and South Pacific oceans. Like an island, it is surrounded by water, but because of its great size, geologists classify it as a continent.

Australian Outback — is the huge interior portion of Australia, a remote area made up mostly of desert and dry grassland.

Emu — a large ostrichlike bird that stands more than five feet in height. Its sturdy legs allow it to run at high speeds on level ground, but its wings cannot help it fly because they are so small.

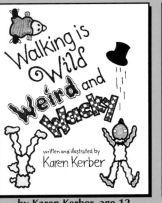

by Karen Kerber, age 12
St. Louis, Missouri
ISBN 0-933849-29-X   Full Color

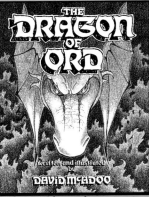

by David McAdoo, age 14
Springfield, Missouri
ISBN 0-933849-23-0   Inside Duotone

by Amy Hagstrom, age 9
Portola, California
ISBN 0-933849-15-X   Full Color

by Isaac Whitlatch, age 11
Casper, Wyoming
ISBN 0-933849-16-8   Full Color

by Leslie Ann MacKeen, age 9
Winston-Salem, North Carolina
ISBN 0-933849-19-2   Full Color

by Elizabeth Haidle, age 13
Beaverton, Oregon
ISBN 0-933849-20-6   Full Color

by Heidi Salter, age 19
Berkeley, California
ISBN 0-933849-21-4   Full Color

by Lauren Peters, age 7
Kansas City, Missouri
ISBN 0-933849-25-7   Full Color

by Aruna Chandrasekhar, age 9
Houston, Texas
ISBN 0-933849-33-8   Full Color

by Anika Thomas, age 13
Pittsburgh, Pennsylvania
ISBN 0-933849-34-6   Inside Two Colors

by Cara Reichel, age 15
Rome, Georgia
ISBN 0-933849-35-4   Inside Two Colors

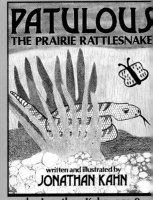

by Jonathan Kahn, age 9
Richmond Heights, Ohio
ISBN 0-933849-36-2   Full Color

by Benjamin Kendall, age 7
State College, Pennsylvania
ISBN 0-933849-42-7   Full Color

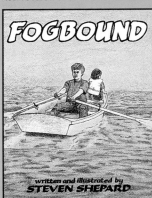

by Steven Shepard, age 13
Great Falls, Virginia
ISBN 0-933849-43-5   Full Color

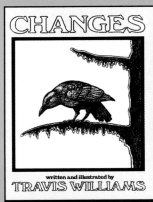

by Travis Williams, age 16
Sardis, B.C., Canada
ISBN 0-933849-44-3   Inside Two Colors

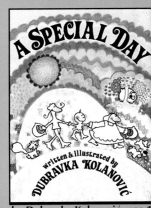

by Dubravka Kolanović, age 1
Savannah, Georgia
ISBN 0-933849-45-1   Full Color

THE NATIONAL WRITTEN & ILLUSTRATED BY...AWARD WINNERS

by Dav Pilkey, age 19
Cleveland, Ohio
ISBN 0-933849-22-2   Full Color

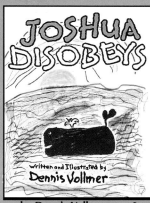

by Dennis Vollmer, age 6
Grove, Oklahoma
ISBN 0-933849-12-5   Full Color

by Lisa Gross, age 12
Santa Fe, New Mexico
ISBN 0-933849-13-3   Full Color

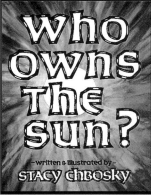

by Stacy Chbosky, age 14
Pittsburgh, Pennsylvania
ISBN 0-933849-14-1   Full Color

by Michael Cain, age 11
Annapolis, Maryland
ISBN 0-933849-26-5   Full Color

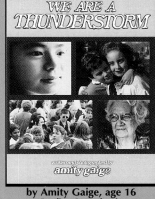

by Amity Gaige, age 16
Reading, Pennsylvania
ISBN 0-933849-27-3   Full Color

by Adam Moore, age 9
Broken Arrow, Oklahoma
ISBN 0-933849-24-9   Inside Duotone

by Michael Aushenker, age 19
Ithaca, New York
ISBN 0-933849-28-1   Full Color

by Jayna Miller, age 19
Zanesville, Ohio
ISBN 0-933849-37-0   Full Color

by Bonnie-Alise Leggat, age 8
Culpepper, Virginia
ISBN 0-933849-39-7   Full Color

by Lisa Kirsten Butenhoff, age 13
Woodbury, Minnesota
ISBN 0-933849-40-0   Full Color

by Jennifer Brady, age 17
Columbia, Missouri
ISBN 0-933849-41-9   Full Color

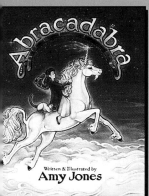

by Amy Jones, age 17
Shirley, Arkansas
ISBN 0-933849-46-X   Full Color

by Shintaro Maeda, age 8
Wichita, Kansas
ISBN 0-933849-51-6   Full Color

by Miles MacGregor, age 12
Phoenix, Arizona
ISBN 0-933849-52-4   Full Color

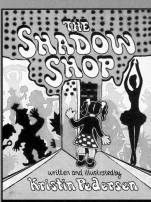

by Kristin Pedersen, age 18
Etobicoke, Ont., Canada
ISBN 0-933849-53-2   Full Color

Travis Williams
age 16

Anika D. Thomas
age 13

Isaac Whitlatch
age 11

Elizabeth Haidle
age 13

Miles MacGregor
age 12

Jayna Miller
age 19

Jonathan Kahn
age 9

Stacy Chbosky
age 14

David McAdoo
age 12

Amity Gaige
age 16

BOOKS FOR STUDENTS BY STUDENTS!

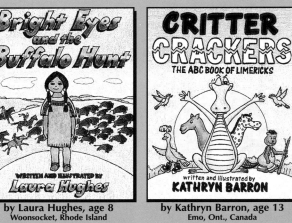

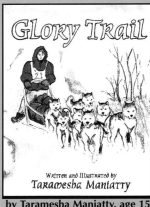
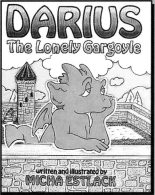
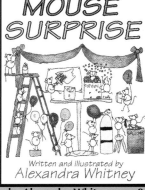

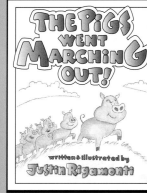
Written & Illustrated by... by David Melton

Written & Illustrated by...
a revolutionary two-brain approach for teaching students how to write and illustrate amazing books
David Melton
96 Pages • Illustrated • Softcover
ISBN 0-933849-00-1

This highly acclaimed teacher's manual offers classroom-proven, step-by-step instructions in all aspects of teaching students how to write, illustrate, assemble and bind original books. Loaded with information and positive approaches that really work. Contains lesson plans, more than 200 illustrations, and suggested adaptations for use at all grade levels – K through college.

The results are dazzling!
– Children's Book Review Service, Inc.

...an exceptional book!
Just browsing through it stimulates excitement for writing.
– Joyce E. Juntune, Executive Director American Creativity Association

A "how-to" book that really works!
– Judy O'Brien, Teacher

WRITTEN & ILLUSTRATED BY... provides current of enthusiasm, positive thinking and faith in the creative spirit of children. David Melton has the heart of a teacher.
– THE READING TEACHER